BRUCE JONES & RICHARD CORBEN

RIP IN TIME

FANTAGOR PRESS
P. O. BOX 8632
KANSAS CITY, MO 64114

816-942-7805

PRINTED IN THE U. S. A.

ISBN 0-9623841-1-9

SECOND PRINTING, JANUARY 1991

FANTAGOR
PRESS
PRESENTS

CRUNCH

SQUEK!

A COJO PRODUCTION

RICHARD CORBEN

BRUCE JONES

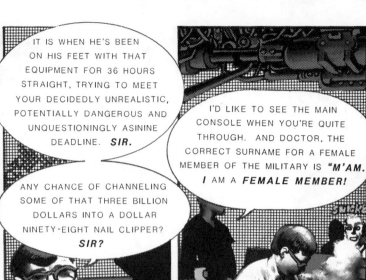

... AS SOON AS I ELIMINATE THIS HANGNAIL FROM MY LIFE.

IT IS WHEN HE'S BEEN ON HIS FEET WITH THAT EQUIPMENT FOR 36 HOURS STRAIGHT, TRYING TO MEET YOUR DECIDEDLY UNREALISTIC, POTENTIALLY DANGEROUS AND UNQUESTIONINGLY ASININE DEADLINE. *SIR.*

I'D LIKE TO SEE THE MAIN CONSOLE WHEN YOU'RE QUITE THROUGH. AND DOCTOR, THE CORRECT SURNAME FOR A FEMALE MEMBER OF THE MILITARY IS *"M'AM."* I AM A *FEMALE MEMBER!*

ANY CHANCE OF CHANNELING SOME OF THAT THREE BILLION DOLLARS INTO A DOLLAR NINETY-EIGHT NAIL CLIPPER? *SIR?*

IS THIS THE WAY A CHIEF ENGINEER SPENDS HIS TIME OVERSEEING THREE BILLION DOLLARS WORTH OF FINELY TUNED, SECRET GOVERNMENT EQUIPMENT?

WELL, I WON'T ARGUE THAT, COLONEL--IF EVER I SAW A FEMALE "MEMBER" YOU'RE IT! RIGHT THIS WAY ... *SIR.*

EVERYTHING'S IN ORDER FOR THE ELEVEN-THIRTY TEST, I ASSUME?

TAKE A LOOK IF YOU DON'T TRUST ME ...

... M-M ... YES, SEEMS YOU'VE KEPT ABREAST OF THE SCHEDULE ...

DOCTOR!

SORRY, MUST HAVE BEEN GETTING A LITTLE *"BEHIND"* IN MY WORK, COLONEL ...

THAT WAS *ADOLESCENT, IRRESPONSIBLE,* AND ... AND ...

"HORNY" IS THE WORD YOU'RE LOOKING FOR. WHY DON'T YOU CLIMB OFF YOUR ICBM FOR FIVE MINUTES AND JOIN ME AT THE COMMISSARY FOR A QUICK ONE?

YOU *DISGUST* ME! (COUGH-COUGH!)

I DISGUST MYSELF. BUT, IMPROBABLE AS IT MAY BE, I HAPPEN TO BELIEVE THERE'S A HUMAN HEART BEATING SOMEWHERE BENEATH ALL THAT SALAD DRESSING PINNED TO YOUR NOT UNAMPLE BOSOM. WHATTYA SAY, COLONEL -- *M'AM* -- A QUICK DRINK WITH OL' DOC PHILPOT BEFORE WE REWRITE HISTORY TOGETHER?

NOT IF YOU WERE THE LAST MAN ON *EARTH!*

OH DEAR, WELL, IN THAT CASE I THINK YOU'D BETTER TAKE A LOOK AT THIS MONITOR, COLONEL; IT COULD STRIP THE ESSENCE OF THE PROJECT BARE ...

THE *PROJECT?* WHAT IS IT? WHAT'S THE MAT--

OH MY GOD!

YOU *DIDN'T!* YOU-YOU -!!

OF COURSE I'M THE ONLY ONE WHO'S VIEWED THIS PARTICULAR VIDEO SO FAR -- I DIDN'T WANT TO CONSULT THE *CREW* UNTIL I'D TALKED TO YOU. UH, WEREN'T WE DISCUSSING SOMETHING ABOUT DRINKS?

ONE DRINK -- *ONE!* -- THEN YOU'LL ERASE IT?

WHATEVER THE COLONEL ORDERS, SIR, M'AM, YOUR HONOR.

I WANT TO BE BACK HERE *BEFORE* THE ELEVEN-THIRTY TEST!

YES , YOUR WORSHIP ...

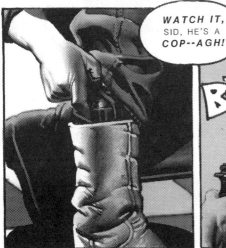

... SID!

DON'T TRY IT, SID!

RIP? ...

BLINK, AND THE LADY EATS STEEL ...

THROW ME THE THIRTY-EIGHT, RAMBO!

AGH!

I MEAN IT, IDIOT-STICK!

ATZA GOOD BOY!

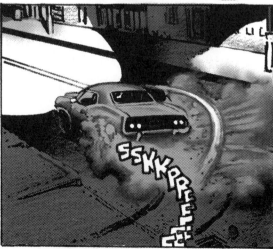

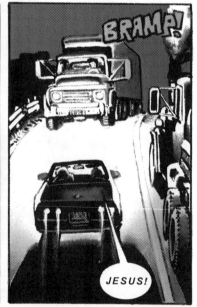

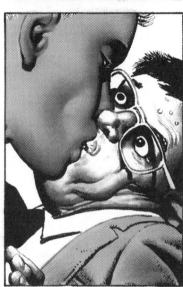

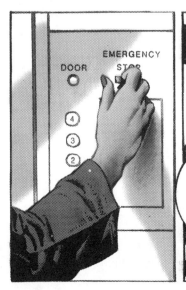

EEE-*HAH!* THERE SHE GOES!

AND JUST IN TIME --HERE COMES YOUR BOYFRIEND!

YOU GOT GOOD TASTE IN BROADS, PAL AND LOUSY TASTE IN CARS! HEY, FOUND MY OLD FORTY-FIVE IN THE GLOVE BOX DID YA?

OKAY, CLIMB OUT SLOWLY, HANDS WHERE I CAN *SEE* THEM!

SORRY, PAL, JUST CAN'T DO THAT ...

EEEEEEE-HAH!

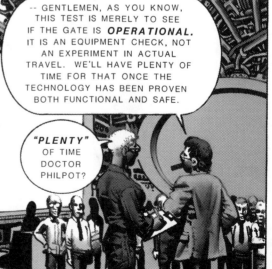

-- GENTLEMEN, AS YOU KNOW, THIS TEST IS MERELY TO SEE IF THE GATE IS *OPERATIONAL.* IT IS AN EQUIPMENT CHECK, NOT AN EXPERIMENT IN ACTUAL TRAVEL. WE'LL HAVE PLENTY OF TIME FOR THAT ONCE THE TECHNOLOGY HAS BEEN PROVEN BOTH FUNCTIONAL AND SAFE.

"PLENTY" OF TIME DOCTOR PHILPOT?

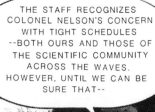

THE STAFF RECOGNIZES COLONEL NELSON'S CONCERN WITH TIGHT SCHEDULES --BOTH OURS AND THOSE OF THE SCIENTIFIC COMMUNITY ACROSS THE WAVES. HOWEVER, UNTIL WE CAN BE SURE THAT--

YES, YES, BUT WE WON'T *BE* SURE UNTIL WE *BEGIN!* GENTLEMEN, I SUGGEST WE PROCEED WITHOUT FURTHER DELAY.

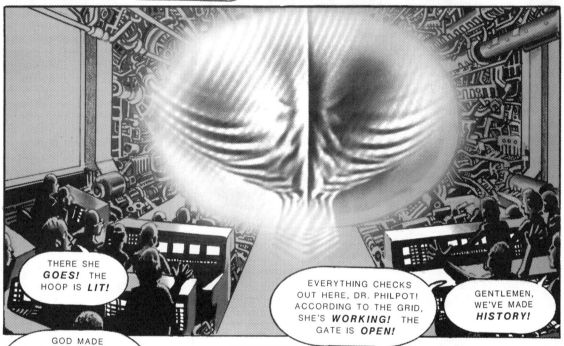

THERE SHE *GOES!* THE HOOP IS *LIT!*

EVERYTHING CHECKS OUT HERE, DR. PHILPOT! ACCORDING TO THE GRID, SHE'S *WORKING!* THE GATE IS *OPEN!*

GENTLEMEN, WE'VE MADE *HISTORY!*

GOD MADE HISTORY, BEACHAM ... WE'RE ONLY TRAMPING AROUND IN IT ...

THAT'S WHY GOD GAVE YOU SUCH BIG, HEALTHY FEET, DOCTOR.

WELL, WELL, SOMETHING'S FINALLY MELTED THE ICE QUEEN, EH PHILPOT?

JUST *LOOK* AT IT! IT'S ALMOST *ALIVE!* ALMOST --ALMOST *SENSUAL...*

GET BACK TO YOUR BOARD, BANKS.

WNAARROO

WHAT'S THAT-- ?

DARLENE?...CAN YOU HEAR ME?...

UH!

(COUGH!-
COUGH)
(HACK!)

PHILPOT?
YOU STILL
THERE?

(COUGH-
COUGH!)

(CRACKLE)
SCULLY? WHAT
HAPPENED?

NEVER MIND THAT,
JUST TELL ME
WHERE WE ARE.

KA WHOOM!

YOU STILL ALIVE, SWEET-BUNS?

YOU **MUST** STAY WHERE YOU ARE, SERGEANT SCULLY! YOU **CAN'T** KNOW THE DANGERS OF THAT ERA!

LOOK, DOC, PREHISTORIC WORLD OR NOT, SOMEBODY MADE OFF WITH MY FIANCEE-- I CAN'T JUST STAND AROUND AND SWAT MOSQUITOS.

AS SOON AS WE REPAIR THE TIME-HOOP, WE'LL SEND SOMEONE **IN** FOR YOU! IT'S **IMPERATIVE** YOU DON'T GO **TRAMPING** AROUND IN--

IS THAT A FIRE?...

...THIRTY-SIX, THIRTY-SEVEN, THIRTY-EIGHT! THAT GLOVE COMPARTMENT OF YOUR BOYFRIENDS HAD A *FULL* BOX! THAT PLUS THE FOUR IN HIS POLICE REVOLVER MAKES FORTY-TWO! WE'RE *WELL ARMED!*

AND ALL HE'S GOT IS WHAT'S LEFT IN THAT OLD .45 OF MINE!

HE'LL KILL YOU ANYWAY...

YEAH? REAL DIRTY HARRY IS HE, YOUR OLD MAN?

HE'S JUST THE BEST COP IN L.A., THAT'S ALL. THE BEST.

SNAP.

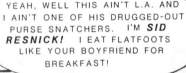

YEAH, WELL THIS AIN'T L.A. AND I AIN'T ONE OF HIS DRUGGED-OUT PURSE SNATCHERS. I'M *SID RESNICK!* I EAT FLATFOOTS LIKE YOUR BOYFRIEND FOR BREAKFAST!

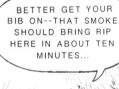

BETTER GET YOUR BIB ON--THAT SMOKE SHOULD BRING RIP HERE IN ABOUT TEN MINUTES...

OH, HE'LL COME ALL RIGHT--ONLY HE WON'T SHOOT CAUSE HIS SASSY LITTLE HIGH-TONE FIANCEE IS GONNA BE RIGHT BY MY SIDE ALL THE TIME!

--AND THE MINUTE HE POKES HIS GREASY LITTLE COPPER HEAD AROUND THE CORNER--

--I BLOW IT OFF HIS GREASY LITTLE COPPER SHOULDERS!

WHAT ARE THEY?

DINOSAURS, WHAT ELSE?

PHILPOT? I'M LOOKING AT A LARGE HERD OF RHINO-LIKE ANIMALS--EXCEPT *BIGGER.* THEY HAVE THREE HORNS AND A KIND OF BONY COLLAR OR SOMETHING. THEY APPEAR TO BE GRAZING.

ARE THEY DANGEROUS?

SOUNDS LIKE TRICERATOPS.

THEY'RE PROBABLY *HERBIVORES,* SCULLY, BUT WE KNOW *NOTHING* ABOUT THEIR TEMPERMENT! I REPEAT: *TURN AROUND NOW* AND HEAD BACK TO *ENTRY POINT, IMMEDIATELY!*

YOU *MUST* OBEY ME! YOU DON'T KNOW WHAT'S *HAPPENING* BACK AT THIS EN--*CLICK!*

YOU SHUT HIM *OFF!*

WE HAVE TO CROSS THE MEADOW TO GET TO THE SMOKE. LET'S GO...

WALK SLOWLY... SHOW NO FEAR... LOOK STRAIGHT AHEAD AND KEEP QUIET...

THIS IS *CRAZY...*

BBOOOOMMMM!

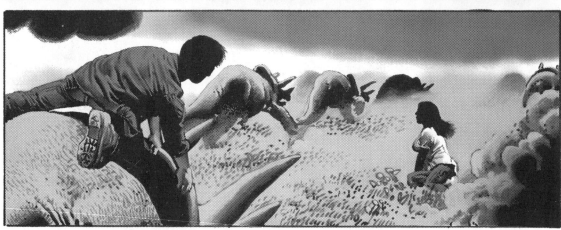

DARLENE!

THUMP THUMP THUMP THUMP

GRAB MY ARM!

THUMP THUMP THUMP THUMP

THUMP THUMP THUMP THUMP THU

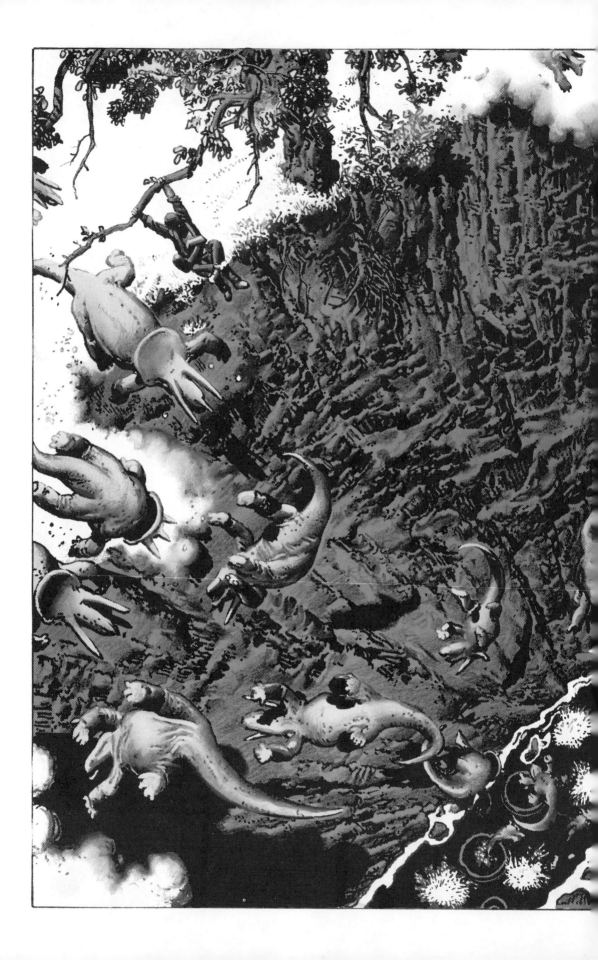

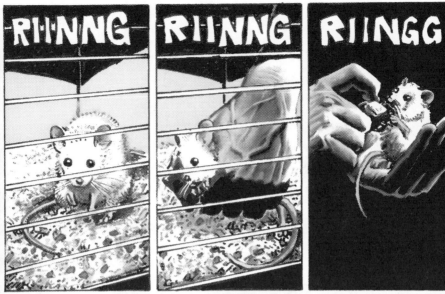

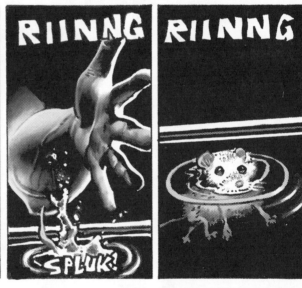

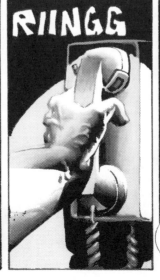

CRUNCH

SKREK!

GRRRR CHOMP
RIPCHOMPCHOMP
GULP!

GOOD MORNING...

MY GOD, IT'S *DAWN!* I SLEPT ALL *NIGHT!*

YOU NEEDED IT. BIG DAY.

YOU SAVED MY LIFE, RIP...

I DON'T THINK I EVER THANKED YOU...

GOTTA GET GOIN... LOSIN' TIME...

C'MON, DARLENE...

SMAK

WHAT THE HELL ARE YOU *DOIN?*

TWMP

UH!

WELL. EX-*CUUUUUZE* ME, MR. *HOT-SHOT L.A. COP!*

I WAS JUST TRYIN TO SHOW A LITTLE *GRATITUDE!* HOPE YOU DIDN'T GET MY *GERMS* OR *NOTHIN!*

I GUESS US LOW-LIFE *STREET TYPES* AIN'T GOT THE *FINESSE* OF YER FANCY *UPTOWN* FIANCEE!

LOOK, I'M SORRY IF--

JUST KEEP YER GREASY COP HANDS *OFF* ME, HUH? JUST FORGET IT EVER *HAPPENED!*

C'MON, LET'S GO FIND YER *PARK AVENUE* GIRL FRIEND IF YER SO GODDAMN ANXIOUS TO GET YERSELF *KILLED!*

--AND BY THE WAY: YOU KISS LIKE A *FRUITCAKE,* YA KNOW THAT?

SPLASH... SPLASH...

SPLASH
SPLASH
SPLASH

SPLASH

SPLASH

WHAT THE HELL ARE YOU *DOIN?*

THANKS FOR THE DOPE--

--I WON'T LET HIM INTO THIS LAB

WAIT!

WELL?

...UH, Y-YOUR 'OFFER' A FEW SECONDS AGO...IS IT STILL GOOD?

ARE YOU SERIOUS?

ENLISTED PEOPLE GET LONELY TOO, DR. PHILPOT...

I DON'T GET IT...

HOW CAN YOU-- STOP! LOOK OUT!

KONK

... YOU MIGHT BUMP YOUR HEAD.

PHILPOT! PHILPOT! WE'RE IN *TROUBLE!*

--PHILPOT, THIS IS SERGEANT SCULLY! DO YOU *COPY?* IS ANYBODY *THERE?*

THAT *RAVINE,* QUICK!

DOWN!

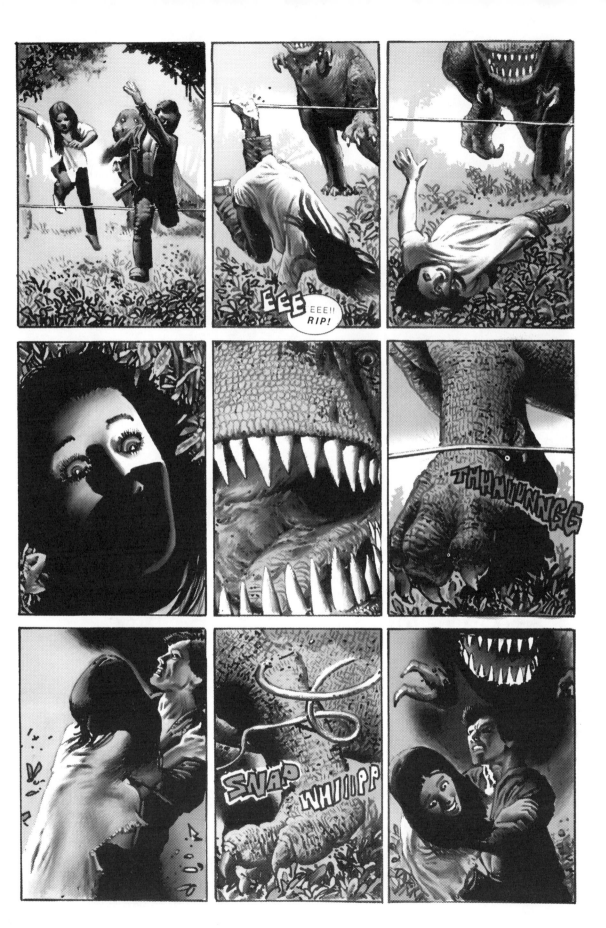

KA-ROOOMMM!

BLAM BLAM BLAM

...IS IT--??

I SINCERELY HOPE SO, THE GUN'S EMPTY...

SNNGGGHHHHHHH

ROPER!

CHRIST, YOU *SCARED* ME!

PHILPOT...?

I *DRUGGED* HIM, HE'LL BE OUT FOR HOURS, WE'LL HAVE TIME.

AS I SAID ON THE PHONE, THE GATE IS *DAMAGED* SLIGHTLY-- I CAN ONLY HOLD IT OPEN FOR YOU A *SECOND* OR TWO.

TAKE THIS--IT'S STILL *EXPERIMENTAL* BUT *DEADLY.*

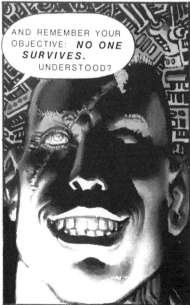

AND REMEMBER YOUR OBJECTIVE: *NO ONE SURVIVES.* UNDERSTOOD?

IT'S *OPEN!* GO! *NOW!*

REEEE-UNK!

RAUGH!

RNN-UNK!

GRRRR

KA THUNN!

POOR THING...

RRUIP

WHO SAYS?

HUH?

WHO **SAYS** YOU COULDN'T ATTAIN THEM? GO GET THEM IF THAT'S WHAT YOU WANT! **TAKE EM!**

YOU MEAN LIKE YOU AND SID? **HMPH!** I GOT THREE GENERATIONS OF GUILT PREVENTING ME FROM THAT!

YER A BRIGHT ENOUGH GUY--YOU COULD HAVE ANYTHING MISS FANCY PANTS HAS.

I'M A COP. IT'S WHAT I DO WELL. I'M NOT MUCH GOOD AT ANYTHING BUT SURVIVING. BESIDES WHICH, I ENJOY IT.

YER A **JERK,** THAT'S WHAT YOU ARE.

IS THAT A FACT?

SHE'LL **DUMP** YOU. I KNOW THE TYPE.

DO YOU NOW?

I MAY BE WHITE TRASH TO YOU, LOVER, BUT I'M STILL A WOMAN.

NOT A VERY **BRIGHT** ONE IF YOU HANG AROUND GARBAGE LIKE SID.

SID IS...JUST A STEPPING STONE.

DARLENE, YOU'RE ALL HEART.

SHM

LOOK, IT AIN'T BEEN EASY FOR **MY** FAMILY NEITHER! YA WANNA HEAR ALL ABOUT THE DRUNKEN FATHER, THE HOOKER MOTHER, THE RAPED KIDS?--OR HAVE YA GOT THE **TIME?**

SKREEK!

YOU **DID** IT! **YOU GOT HIM!**

ONE NIGHT HE CAME HOME DRUNKER THAN USUAL. HE BEAT MY MOTHER TO DEATH. I STOOD THERE SCREAMIN, *TEARIN* AT HIM AND HE BEAT HER TO DEATH... SHE WAS CARRYIN HIS FIFTH CHILD...

HE'S AT JOLIET, SERVING A LIFE SENTENCE. I HAVEN'T SEEN HIM SINCE THAT NIGHT... THAT NIGHT I SWORE I WAS *NEVER* GOING TO END UP LIKE MY MOTHER...I WAS GOING TO HAVE *MONEY, PLENTY* OF MONEY...

THERE WAS A WHOLE TWENTY-SEVEN DOLLARS IN THAT LIQUOR STORE REGISTER.

ALL RIGHT, I'VE BEEN *STUPID!* SID WAS A *MISTAKE! THERE!* I *SAID* IT! YA *HAPPY?*

YOU AIN'T EXACTLY A PARAGON OF *VIRTUE* YERSELF, OFFICER SCULLY! LETTIN YERSELF BE *KEPT* BY SOME VASSAR SLUT WHO CAN'T GET TURNED ON UNLESS IT'S WITH A WORKING CLASS--

SLAP

THE *LAST* PERSON WHO DID THAT WAS MY FATHER...

KRAK!

EE-HAUGH!

Y-YOU...YOU **BLINDED** THE THING!

HA-HA! SERVES IT **RIGHT** FOR BEIN SO **STUPID!** HA-HA!

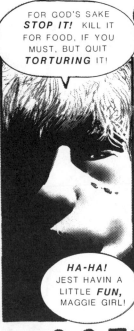

FOR GOD'S SAKE **STOP IT!** KILL IT FOR FOOD, IF YOU MUST, BUT QUIT **TORTURING** IT!

HA-HA! JEST HAVIN A LITTLE **FUN,** MAGGIE GIRL!

YOU'RE AN **ANIMAL!**

YEAH? MEBE SO. BUT YOU **LIKE** ANIMALS, DON'T YA MAGGIE GIRL? SPECIALLY IN THE **SACK!**

HEY **LOOK!** I'M A **TOREADOR!** HA-HA! I'M A FRIGGIN **TOREADOR!**

--AND NOW, FOR THE **DEATH BLOW!**

WHOOM!

WHAT TH--?

W-WHAT HAPPENED?

DUNNO...SOMETHIN **MOVIN** IN THE BRUSH OVER THERE...

ZAT **YOU** IN THERE, COPPER? HEH-HEH! YOU BRING ALONG A **BAZOOKA** OR SOMETHIN?

ECK!

TWAP!

C-C-C-C-C!

-C-

Y-YOU... *KILLED* HIM!

TH KLUM PH

NO. I *NEED* HIM, TO SUMMON THE POLICEMAN.

RIP? *WHY?* WHAT ARE-- WHO *ARE* YOU?

I AM A *HUNTER,* LIKE YOUR FIANCE. AND LIKE YOUR FIANCE, I TAKE BOTH PRIDE AND PLEASURE IN MY WORK--NOT LIKE THIS BUMBLING AMATEUR HERE. HIS KIND IS NO MATCH FOR MEN LIKE SCULLY AND MYSELF.

W-WHO SENT YOU? WHAT'RE YOU GOING TO DO?

IT'S RARE THAT I FIND AN OPPORTUNITY TO COMPETE WITH A FELLOW HUNTER OF YOUR FIANCE'S CALIBRE. IT WILL BE AN HONOR, A PLEASURE AND A *CHALLENGE.*

AND JOHN ROPER *ALWAYS* ACCEPTS A CHALLENGE...

Y-YOU WERE SENT HERE TO *KILL* US! *WHY?*

SOMETHING ABOUT DISTURBING THE TEMPORAL STRUCTURE OF THE SPACE-TIME CONTINUUM--IT'S OF NO CONSEQUENCE TO ME. I ACCEPTED MERELY TO HAVE THE CHANCE AT COMBAT WITH SERGEANT SCULLY...

VERY *NEAT,* COLONEL NELSON! DOES YOUR PSYCHOPATH *KNOW* YOU'RE MONITORING HIM?

PHILPOT! WELL... HAVE A NICE NAP? NO, MR. ROPER WAS NOT INFORMED OF THAT.

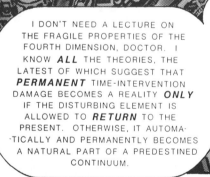

IT WON'T WORK, YOU KNOW-- EVEN IF ROPER KILLS THE OTHERS, THEY MAY *ALREADY* HAVE CAUSED IRREPARABLE DAMAGE, BREAKING OPEN THE *ENTROPIC CHANNEL,* ALLOWING THE INCALCULABLE FORCES OF TEMPORAL PROGRESSION TO *DIFFUSE* ACROSS AN INFINITE SPECTRUM OF PROGRESSIVELY *WEAKER* MATRIXES. BY PHYSICALLY *TOUCHING* THE PAST, THEY COULD HAVE ALREADY *ALTERED* THE PRESENT...

I DON'T NEED A LECTURE ON THE FRAGILE PROPERTIES OF THE FOURTH DIMENSION, DOCTOR. I KNOW *ALL* THE THEORIES, THE LATEST OF WHICH SUGGEST THAT *PERMANENT* TIME-INTERVENTION DAMAGE BECOMES A REALITY *ONLY* IF THE DISTURBING ELEMENT IS ALLOWED TO *RETURN* TO THE PRESENT. OTHERWISE, IT AUTOMA-TICALLY AND PERMANENTLY BECOMES A NATURAL PART OF A PREDESTINED CONTINUUM.

THESE FIVE TRAVELERS MAY WELL BE OUR GREAT ANCESTORS, BUT AS LONG AS THEY STAY PUT IN THE CRETACEOUS, WE NEED HAVE NO FEAR OF THEM.

"STAY PUT!" --BUT THEN WHAT ABOUT *ROPER?* HE AGREED TO REMAIN THERE?

...*I SEE!* HE DOESN'T *KNOW* IT'S A ONE-WAY TRIP! BUT IF THEY'RE REALLY NOT DANGEROUS TO THE FUTURE, TUCKED AWAY THERE IN THE PAST, WHY KILL THEM AT ALL?

THERE WILL BE *FUTURE* TRIPS, DOCTOR...

OF COURSE...AND THESE FIVE WAYFARERS MIGHT PROVE PROBLEMATIC IN THEIR EAGERNESS TO HITCH A RIDE BACK! WELL, YOU'VE CERTAINLY THOUGHT OF EVERYTHING!

WHERE *IS* EVERYBODY? WHAT HAPPENED TO THE SECOND SHIFT?

OH?

SOME OPERATIONS, DOCTOR, ARE BEST KEPT SECRET FROM EVEN THE MEMBERS OF ELITE PERSONNEL.

INCLUDING *THIS* MEMBER, I SEE...

REGRETTABLY, YES, DOCTOR. TAKE HIM TO HIS ROOM...WE'LL DEAL WITH HIM LATER.

AND WHO KILLS THE SLAVES THAT KILLED THE SLAVES THAT BUILT KING TUT'S TOMB, COLONEL NELSON?

GOOD NIGHT, DOCTOR. I'M *SORRY* IT HAD TO COME TO THIS.

OH, EXCUSE ME...

COUGH!

ARAOUGH!

OOWH!

MAKE A MOVE AND I TAKE HER *HEAD* OFF!

YOU CAN'T POSSIBLY FREE YOUR FIANCEE, SERGEANT SCULLY, UNLESS I SHOW YOU WHICH ROPE TO PULL ...

I SHALL BE HONORED TO DO THAT *AFTER* YOU'VE AGREED TO JOIN ME IN A GAME OF JUNGLE COMBAT--JUST THE TWO OF US--TWO PREMORDIAL HUNTERS, ENACTING THE OLDEST, NOBELEST LAW OF NATURE: *KILL OR BE KILLED!*

WHAT DO YOU SAY, SERGEANT? I KNOW YOU'RE ACHING AS I AM TO SEE WHICH OF US IS THE BETTER HUNTER. UP TO NOW NEITHER OF US.HAS BEEN BEATEN AT OUR PROFESSIONS ... IT IS THE *ULTIMATE* TEST OF OUR CAREERS ...

WILL YOU ACCEPT MY CHALLENGE?

YOU'RE NUTS.

... (SOB!) ... OH RIP! ... (SOB!) *HELP* ME!

LIE QUIETLY ... DON'T MOVE UNTIL I TELL YOU ...

HEH-HEH! ... THE *GORDIAN KNOT,* EH, SCULLY?

... THREE, FOUR, FIVE ... RIGHT ...

RIP! BE *CAREFUL!*

THE ROPES ARE LOOSE NOW, BUT *DON'T MOVE* UNTIL I GIVE THE SIGNAL-- THEN JUMP INTO MY ARMS WITH ALL *ALL* YOUR STRENGTH!

NOW!

"*MALAYAN SPEAR MAZE*" FIRST DESCRIBED IN ALTMAN'S BOOK, *TRIBAL WARFARE OF THE ANCIENTS,* RANDOM HOUSE, 1946.

REMARKABLE! EVEN BETTER THAN I'D HOPED! NOW, IF WE COULD--

YOU'RE UNDER ARREST FOR THE MURDER OF SID RESNICK. YOU HAVE THE RIGHT TO REMAIN SILENT. ANYTHING YOU SAY CAN AND WILL BE--

HAW! HAW! I SHOULD HAVE KNOWN! THE *DEDICATED* L. A. COP! VERY WELL THEN, *ARREST* ME! --

--BUT *CATCH* ME FIRST! *HAW! HAW! HAW! HAW!*

SWAT

OWH!

FIFTH AVENUE SLUT!

GET YOUR HANDS OFF ME!

STOP IT! YOU WANT HIM TO HEAR US?

I WON'T BE BELITTLED THIS WAY RIP! STAY OUT HERE AND PLAY YOUR STUPID WARRIOR GAMES IF YOU MUST--I'M FINDING A WAY BACK TO CIVILIZATION!

MAGGIE! I SAID STAY BEHIND ME!

SNAP

SWIP

AGH!

MISSED HER-- WHAT A PITY.

THEY'RE AS GOOD AS DEAD, DR. PHILPOT. THERE'S NOTHING YOU CAN DO FROM HERE. PLEASE OPEN THE DOOR AND STOP ALL THIS NONSENSE!

--AS FOR THE Z-27 UNIFLYER, IT WAS NEVER TESTED AND FOR THAT MATTER, NEVER COMPLETED. FLYING IT WOULD BE SUICIDAL. ARE YOU *LISTENING* TO ME, DR. PHILPOT?

I'M WELL AWARE OF Z-27'S VIRTUES, COL. NELSON--I HELPED *INSTALL* THEM, REMEMBER? IT WAS I WHO FIRST PROPOSED A BACK-UP SYSTEM FOR CONTACT-FREE TIME TRAVEL SHOULD THE X-54 FAIL. --APPARENTLY IT HAS FAILED, COLONEL.

ROPER WILL KILL THEM ALL, DOCTOR. HE'S AN EXPERT. YOU'LL NEVER REACH THEM IN TIME.

AH, BUT MY DEAR COL. NELSON, *"TIME"* IS THE OPERATIVE WORD!

MAGGIE! GRAB MY HAND!

... (GASP!) ... (PANT!) ... AH-H-H-H ...

(GASP!) ... (CHOKE!) ...

WHY?

BEATS ME ... (PANT!) ... MAYBE I GOT TO FEELIN' *SORRY* FOR YOU, WHAT WITH ALL THEM WASTED WEDDING INVITATIONS...

DO YOU THINK HE WENT OVER?

RIP? NAW. HE'S AROUND, SOMEWHERE. RIP'S A SURVIVOR.

YOU'RE *BOTH* SURVIVORS, AREN'T YOU? FUNNY THING IS: *I'M* NOT. RIP MERELY *WANTS* MONEY-- I *NEED* IT.

I KNOW.

I ENVY YOU, DARLENE...

DON'T. DON'T ENVY ANYBODY. IT'S A WASTE OF A GOOD LIFE.

WORDS TO LIVE BY ...

UNFORTUNATELY, LIFE IS SUCH A *TENUOUS* THING, ISN'T IT?

WELL, IF IT ISN'T THE LOCAL PSYCHO.

COME JOIN ME LADIES, THE PARTY'S JUST GETTING UNDERWAY!

WHEN I GIVE THE WORD, *RUN!*

NO! YOU SICK SON OF A B--

IF THE GOOD SERGEANT DID INDEED SURVIVE THE FLOOD, HE SHOULD EVENT-UALLY COME THIS WAY, FOLLOWING MY TRACKS. WHEN HE SEES HIS DEAD FIANCEE HERE IN THE CLEARING, HE WILL REACT ONE OF *TWO* WAYS--*HEART-SICK* AND *CARELESS,* IF HE TRULY LOVES HER--*SHOCKED* BUT *CAUTIOUS* IF HE DOES NOT...

IF HE REACTS THE *FIRST* WAY, HE'LL RUSH *RECKLESSLY* TOWARD HER AND I'LL KILL HIM FROM AMBUSH... IF HE REACTS THE *SECOND* WAY, THEN HIS HEART OBVIOUSLY BELONGS TO YOU, AND THE HUNT GOES ON!

A NECESSARY *STRATAGEM* TO DISTRACT SERGEANT SCULLY. YOU SHOULD FIND THE RESULTS DOUBLY INTERESTING, MISS DARLENE...

EITHER WAY, WE *BOTH* WIN! HAW, HAW! INTERESTING SITUATION, NO?

TWO DOWN, TWO TO GO, DOCTOR! I TOLD YOU ROPER WOULD KILL THEM ALL! NOW PLEASE OPEN THIS DOOR AT ONCE BEFORE YOU GET YOUR-SELF KILLED AS WELL!

WE'LL BE THROUGH THE DOOR IN *LESS* THAN AN HOUR, DR. PHILPOT...IT WILL GO EASIER ON YOU IF YOU COMPLY NOW!

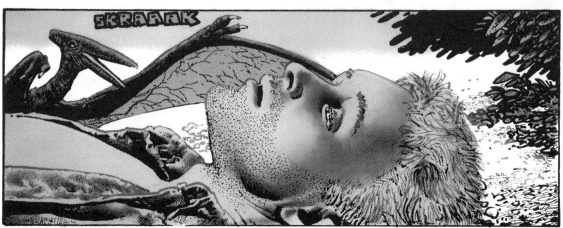

SKRAAAK

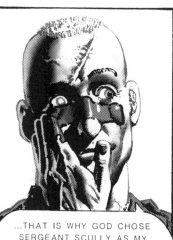

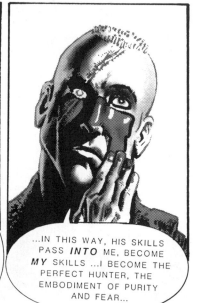

THAT IS HOW LIFE *REPLENISHES* ITSELF:

DRINKING FROM THE WELL OF *DEATH*...

AGGH!

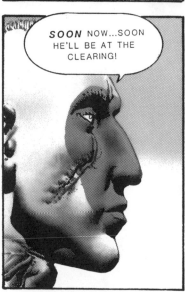

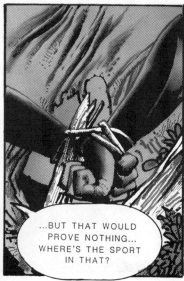

...IT MUST BE ONLY THE *TWO* OF US...

...WITH WEAPONS WE HAVE FASHIONED FROM *NATURE!*

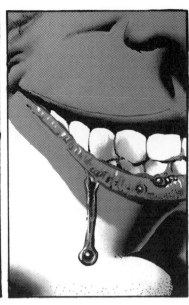

MAGGIE!!

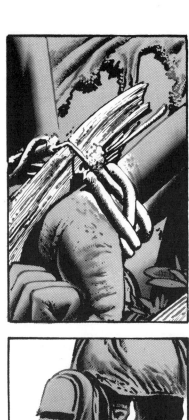

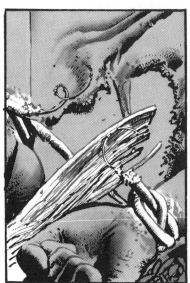
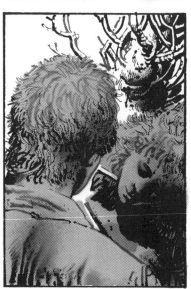

RIP!!
IT'S A
TRAP!!

THUMMMMM

THOK

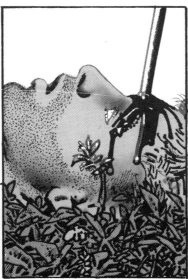

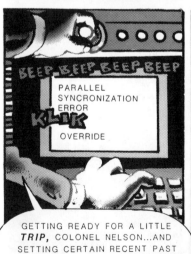

KA RUNNCH

I'M GOING *BACK* FOR HER, DARLENE...

WHO? *MAGGIE?* SHE'S *DEAD!*

NOT IF WE GO BACK AND GET TO HER BEFORE ROPER DOES. ALL WE HAVE TO DO IS SNEAK BACK INTO THAT CONTROL ROOM AND GET THAT HOOP OPERATING AGAIN!

KA PHRUUMM

OH, THAT'S *ALL* WE GOTTA DO, HUH? WELL, WHY DON'T WE JUST GO BACK AND SAVE ABE LINCOLN AND JACK KENNEDY AND JOHN LENNON WHILE WE'RE AT IT?

OKAY. BUT MAGGIE FIRST.

YOU RAN TO HER IN THE CLEARING...YOU STILL *LOVE* HER...

I STILL *CARE* ABOUT HER, DUMMY! *YOU'RE* THE ONE I LOVE! BUT I GOT MAGGIE INTO THIS, AND MAYBE THAT PHILPOT GUY TOO. WE OWE IT TO THEM, DARLENE. WILL YOU HELP ME?

...(SIGH!)...CAN WE HAVE DINNER FIRST? I'M STARVED!

YOU GOT IT!

FOOD

THE END